Voices

by

Richard Lortz

Baker's Plays
c/o Samuel French, Inc.
45 West 25 Street
New York, NY 10010
bakersplays.com

VOICES
ISBN 978-0-87440-457-9
309-B

VOICES

A One-Act Play

For Three Women and Two Men

CHARACTERS

ROBERT WILLIAMS . . . . A young executive

CLAIRE WILLIAMS . . . . His lovely wife

THE MOTHER . . . . An ethereal person

JESSICA . . . . Her daughter; about twelve

JOHN . . . . Jessica's younger brother

TIME: The present.

PLACE: The living room of an old New England mansion.

PRODUCTION NOTES

Since both the story and its emotional impact are in no way dependent upon scenery, this play can be presented against a curtain background, using one or two very simple props, lights, sound effects, costumes and, if feasible, introductory or other music to create the appropriate atmosphere. However, should scenery be desired, a brief description of a possible one-interior set is included in the script.

VOICES

Scene I

SCENE: A shadowed room dominated by a large background window. A fireplace L is equipped with an orange-glow dimmer. Furniture; principally a couch, round table and chairs, a large clock; is covered with dust sheets. The stage should be arranged so that there are two main playing areas: the couch near the fireplace; and at the opposite end of the stage, the table with three upright chairs. Any additional props and furniture are optional and can be added as desired. Exits include: 1] leading in and out of the house, 2] upstairs, 3] the basement, 4] dining and other rooms of the house.

AT RISE OF CURTAIN: The sound of the wind wailing is clearly heard. It is late afternoon.

ROBERT. [Offstage] Claire--! Claire--! Are you coming? The key's in my pocket. The left. Got it?
CLAIRE. [Offstage] Yes!

[ROBERT enters, as if escaping a considerable snow storm, carrying a box of groceries. The box also contains a thermos of hot coffee and paper cups. CLAIRE follows with a small suitcase. Both are dressed for winter. AD LIB whatever is appropriate as they stamp feet, remove hats, gloves, etc., each winded and laughing.]

CLAIRE. [Between breaths, peering from the window] We've never had snow like this before -- never!
ROBERT. [Winded] Maybe next time we'll believe the storm

warnings. Oh! That hill took ten years off my life.

CLAIRE. Well, thank God we made it! Another hour and . . . well, we could have died out there! I can't see the car! It's covered already; there's a drift piling up a mile high!

ROBERT. There's a shovel in the trunk. I can dig us out if I have to. At least it got us here.

CLAIRE. But what about my other case? My night things are in it, and the sleeping pills.

ROBERT. Oh? Well, I'm sorry. Or am I? I can't see how two sleeping pills a night does anyone any good. You're not worried? Not really?

CLAIRE. Aren't you? No one knows we're here -- not even Mother, you made sure of that. Robert, we're fools! Couldn't we, literally -- be buried alive? Tell me -- does it ever cover whole houses?

ROBERT. [Teasing] Yes. Yes, it does. And it doesn't melt until spring; then they carry out the corpses, in perfect shape, but stiff as a board, because they've been frozen all winter. Now stop your nonsense and help me with this mess. I've lost half the groceries. Good Lord, there's a crack in the wine bottle. Do you suppose we can drink it? You have to be careful of glass . . . you swallow even a tiny bit and it cuts your insides to pieces; it makes holes in your descending and transverse colon. [No reaction] Look at that face! How can you be so silly about a snowstorm?

CLAIRE. I told you to turn back; I warned you!

ROBERT. Well, my darling, you warned me a good ten miles too late. If we'd turned back then, we'd still be out there -- buried in the car.

CLAIRE. [Rubs her wrists] Well, I'm not sure it makes a difference. A car or a house, we're still buried. [Between long pauses, as she walks about with distaste and apprehension] No electricity. No telephone. No heat -- except that fireplace, if we can find any wood. Nothing. An empty, dismal house. Can't even see Cape Cod in this weather.

ROBERT. [Somewhat cheerfully] One big pile of 19th Century junk -- fifty million miles from nowhere. All ours -- thanks to you.

CLAIRE. You blame **me** for an inheritance!

ROBERT. Well, why didn't you sell it?

CLAIRE. Oh, good heavens! Sell it! Who in his right mind would buy it? **This** place? Besides, you wanted me to keep it; you know you did.

ROBERT. Of course. And I still do. [Going to her] I want you to interest yourself in anything at all that will help. Because I want my wife back. You're almost well now, Claire; you **are**. Believe me. [SOUND: A disturbance, such as a very faint, errie jangle. Only CLAIRE hears it.]

CLAIRE. Am I? [Looking up and around] Then, why do I feel like this?

ROBERT. Like what?

CLAIRE. Like I don't belong here?

ROBERT. Where? In this **house**? Darling, no one **belongs** here, unless it's Count Dracula or the Bride of Frankenstein. It's a nightmare, I agree, but we can change all that; that's half the fun. Hey, a week ago you couldn't sleep -- thinking about this place, and all the things you were going to do to it.

CLAIRE. [Grimly] **Do** to it. There's only one thing this place needs.

ROBERT. [Anticipating something good] What's that?

CLAIRE. A match. [Pause] I can't live here -- not this summer, not ever.

ROBERT. [Drained of life] I see. What is it this time? Another . . . whim, more self-indulgence in your morbid sensitivity?

CLAIRE. Robert, I'm tired and hungry and cold. I'm chilled right through. Why are you standing there -- asking questions. Can't you start a fire? Can't you do that much? [She rubs her wrists again.]

ROBERT. [Striding to her] Yes! I can do **that** much . . . if **you'd** stop doing **that**! [He separates her hands.]

CLAIRE. [Startled] Oh. I'm sorry. [Looks at, touches her wrists.] I must do it unconsciously. I read somewhere that scars, scar tissue, that is . . .

ROBERT. Okay! Just . . . try not to do it. Well, there's a log here! That helps. [Goes to basement door.]

CLAIRE. [Hating herself] I do try; I do. [Sharply] Where are you going?

ROBERT. [Stingingly polite] To the basement, my darling . . to look for paper and tinder. I can't stick a match under a log.

CLAIRE. I don't want to be left alone.

ROBERT. [Pause, suspiciously] Well, then, come along.

CLAIRE. I'm not going down there.

ROBERT. [With a hiss of exasperation] I can just **see** the good times we're going to have. Look, Claire, think about it this way: it's one hell of a storm, right? Probably the worst blizzard of the century. But it's magnificent, and maybe it can be fun -- even for us -- if we try. Okay? [Pause] Okay? [Pause] Claire? [Long pause. Furiously] **Claire!**

CLAIRE. [Strident] What is it you want? What are we supposed to do -- throw snowballs? . . . play house and curl up like newlyweds? Do you think I want that? Yes, I do. That's why I'm here. I hoped we could find something we lost . . . **not an end to us, Bob, a beginning.** [A quick glance about] But how can I do **anything** . . . think, talk, feel, listen . . . in this house? Don't you **know** that? There's something wrong with it -- **wrong.** [She shudders] I'm crawling all over. And if **you** don't feel it, you're as blunt as a hammer; you always have been. There isn't a shred of sensitivity in you. You have no nerves, and fewer sensibilities.

ROBERT. [Pause, trying to suppress his fury] In that case . . . let's . . . just . . . do things **your** way. We'll put our things back on and go out. I always wanted to die in a blizzard.

CLAIRE. [Puts her arms about him] Bob, don't, please. Try

to understand. Help me.

ROBERT. Help you! God help me! I'm the one who needs it. It's starting all over again, isn't it, Claire . . . fear, anxiety, neurotic fantasy . . . [As he goes to the basement door] . . . half of it -- real, the other half, I'd swear -- fake. [At the door] Are you coming? [She shakes her head. Pause, somewhat gentler] I'll . . . leave the door open.

[The moment ROBERT exits, CLAIRE moves as if to follow him, then stops. She stares out the window, then faces the room. She looks up and around, as she slowly advances center stage, an expression of expectancy and straining-to-hear look on her face. The first manifestation is brief -- extremely faint, a remote spangle of mixed voices, principally laughter. A second similar manifestation follows after a brief pause. CLAIRE stands rigid, only her head turning slowly.]

THE MOTHER. [Off, faint but very clear] John! John! Where are you? John, come here.

JESSICA. [Off] He's in the garden, Mother.

CLAIRE. [Pause. Harshly, strained] Who's there?! Who is it?!

[ROBERT reenters with paper and tinder.]

ROBERT. Boo!

CLAIRE. [Snaps] Robert, stop that! [ROBERT fusses under the next few lines, lighting a fire. CLAIRE broods by the window.]

ROBERT. [After a moment] Sorry, honey.

CLAIRE. No matter what you say, this isn't just a storm, you know; and this isn't just a house.

ROBERT. Well, if it helps any, I share none of your anxieties . . . . neither about the storm, which is rough, but that's about all . . . nor about the house, certainly not about the house . .

I haven't the vaguest notion what you're talking about. I'll tell you one thing, though, I'm bored already. Aren't you? We could play a game. 'Ghost' anyone? 'Twenty Questions?' Shall we recite? You're good at poems. **I know!** -- Give me a line, any line from a Shakespeare play, and I'll tell you exactly what scene and who says it.

THE VOICE. [From off laughs faintly. CLAIRE looks up, then at ROBERT. He's heard nothing.]

ROBERT. [Distressed by her behavior] Claire -- If you . . . **hear** something, or sense something . . . strange in this house, it's coming straight out of you; not . . . [Gesturing about] . . out of wood and stone. [Pause. Softening] You know what the doctor said; you must **want** to get well, not go on . . . [His voice dies.]

CLAIRE. I want to get well. How can you say that? To make me more ashamed? Do you think I **like** behaving like this? One relapse, then another, then . . . [Touching and looking at her wrists] I try. I try so hard. [She goes to him; they hold each other.] This house sounded so beautiful at first. I had the feeling that if ever I got well again, really well, it would be here, this summer. I had so much hope, so many plans . . .

ROBERT. You're trembling. What is it? What's frightening you, Claire?

CLAIRE. Nothing. Just the cold. [Hugging him] Hold me. Hold me. Crush the badness out of me.

JESSICA. [Off. Faint, Eerie] Rain, rain . . . go a-way . . .

CLAIRE. [Hearing the VOICE, struggling to free herself as ROBERT tries to kiss her.] Stop it!

ROBERT. [Surprised, puzzled] What's the matter?

CLAIRE. Don't!

ROBERT. [Attempting to reinstate the embrace] Claire --

CLAIRE. [Shrilly] No! Don't -- touch me! [She frees herself] I don't enjoy being -- **pawed** . . . in dirty corners of empty houses! [Stunned, shocked, ROBERT steps back, in rage kicks over a chair and starts to exit. CLAIRE stops him with --] Why are you going upstairs?

ROBERT. [Sharp, angry] I want to look around.

CLAIRE. At what?

ROBERT. At the house! At **what**! Do you want me to find out what's wrong with it? You hear something, that's for sure. [Heavy sarcasm] Well, maybe there's a squirrel in the attic, scratching its tiny feet against dead leaves and empty nutshells . . . **inaudible**, of course, to someone whose nerves are as dull as mine.

THE VOICES. [Off. Faint laughter.]

JESSICA. [Off. Eerie, remote] Rain, rain, go a-way . . . come again some oth-er day . . . [SOUND: A faint, rhythmic thudding begins, remains a few seconds, fades.]

ROBERT. [Worried by CLAIRE's 'listening,' at the same time, teasing] Why don't you come with me? I'll hold your hand . . . . [Mock eloquence] . . and we shall dispel, dissipate, erase, cast out of every room, the mind's created phantoms.

THE VOICES. [Off. Faint laughter.]

ROBERT. [Now determined to get to the bottom of it.] Claire -- What do you **mean** by **wrong**? Come on, you've got a large enough vocabulary . . .

CLAIRE. [Savage] By **wrong** . . . I mean **evil, sick** . . . containing essences and . . . and dislocations that are incompatible with all that's **normal, healthy, good!**

ROBERT. [Astonished] And that's what you heard -- **dislocations, essences?**

CLAIRE. Yes!

ROBERT. Well! For a minute ya had me worried.

[He exits quickly.]

CLAIRE. Bob! [She moves to follow him, but cannot bring herself to exit. She rubs her wrists, hugs herself, trying to suppress her anger, frustration, panic. She keeps looking up and around, creating a sense of waiting, expect-

ancy. Her fear grows. She finally 'faces' the room with --]
No . . . . . no . . . .

JESSICA. [Off, accompanied by a rhythmic thudding] Rain, rain, go a-way. [Pause, reciting] Once a lonely wizard, while walking by the shore . . .

[CLAIRE isolates the voice and sound as coming from the exit door, R. She crosses fearfully, pushes door open, backs away from what she sees, stopping far L. The thudding suddenly stops, and a large grey ball bounces from inside the door across the stage. JESSICA enters in search of ball. She is a little girl about nine to twelve, entirely grey or colorless. She finds the ball, bounces it twice, pauses, looks out of window, begins to recite a poem to herself aloud.]

Once a lonely wizard, while walking by the shore,
Happened on a Princess, all dress-ed in velour.
[Pause, looks around briefly as if something puzzled her. Lights begin to dim, except on CLAIRE and JESSICA.]
At first he thought of fleeing, but took her hand instead . . .
'Dear Princess, dress-ed in velour; it's you I'd like to wed.'
'How kind, dear sir . . .' [She curtsies] '. . . that would be nice,'
the Princess promptly said . .
[Pause, her voice dropping, slowly]
'Alas, my Lord, I must decline --
Because . . . you see . . . I'm dead.'

THE MOTHER. [Off] Jessica! Jessica!

JESSICA. Yes! I'm coming. [To herself] In a minute. [Pause. Something in the room disturbs her. She keeps looking. Finally she faces, but does not see, CLAIRE crouched fearfully against a wall. Softly --]
Because . . . you see . . . I'm dead.'

TABLEAU. BLACKOUT.

SCENE II

AT RISE OF CURTAIN: ROBERT is on the couch, awakening from sleep. CLAIRE stands by the window.

ROBERT. [Groggy] Good morning.
CLAIRE. Good morning.
ROBERT. [Yawning] How is it? Bad as ever?
CLAIRE. Worse.
ROBERT. [Going to her] How do you feel? Better? You look it. Did you sleep?
CLAIRE. A little.
ROBERT. [He kisses her.] But you **do** -- feel better.
CLAIRE. [A bit irritable] How -- 'better' can I feel? Yes! It's daylight. That helps. And now -- the house is quiet.
ROBERT. [Hesitant] You didn't -- That is -- sorry if I ask . .
CLAIRE. Ask!
ROBERT. Well, the . . . voices you heard. I thought it might be a kind of nightmare. We all have them.
CLAIRE. [Piqued] Do we! That's so generous of you. You live in such a simple world, Robert . . .
ROBERT. Look, I'm not even awake yet.
CLAIRE. A house is a house . . . I don't know if I envy you or pity you. Tell me -- Does the rose on your mother's grave smell as sweet as the rose on your wedding day?
ROBERT. You do feel better.
CLAIRE. Well, if I do, it's because -- I told you -- the house is empty now. They've gone.
ROBERT. [Unable to resist] You mean -- they're out there -- in this blizzard?!
CLAIRE. [Suffering exquisitely] I don't know **where** they are. It can't be a matter of space, time, location as we know it. [Pause] I heard them . . . just a little while this morning. They were going out. [Quietly, afraid of ROBERT's ridicule.] It's . . . raining there, and there was some -- fuss

about raincoats and umbrellas. [Pause] The little boy . . .

ROBERT. Go on.

CLAIRE. The little boy . . . lost his rubbers. They could only find one . . . one rubber.

ROBERT. [Fascinated, almost believing] Did you hear where they were going?

CLAIRE. Yes. They were going to a church and then to a cemetary. The children had fresh flowers, to put on their daddy's grave.

ROBERT. The dead bury the dead. What else? Go on.

CLAIRE. No. But -- There was so much laughing!

ROBERT. [Mock surprise] No tears, no sadness. Anybody dragging a chain, or carrying his head in his hands?

CLAIRE. Don't tease me, Robert! It's all true. It's possible, you know . . . I mean, I **could** have psychic power; maybe I'm a . . . medium.

ROBERT. [Possible but ridiculous] Well, you're good at Ouiji Boards -- you and your mother -- and that other crazy thing . . . up at Harry's farm.

CLAIRE. The divining rod! I **did** find water. [Acting it out] The fork twisted; it turned in my hands!

ROBERT. And now you're projecting voices. AM or FM?

CLAIRE. [Stung, hurt] Oh, Bob! -- don't.

ROBERT. Light of my life, don't lose your sense of humor. Laughter always saved us; maybe it'll save us now.

CLAIRE. Save us! Laughter is a disease. Didn't I ever tell you . . . when I was at the hospital, there was a woman whose sickness was laughter. She lost thirty-two pounds, laughing. Everything was funny to her . . . the chairs, the doors, the bars on the windows. She couldn't stand or walk; they had to wheel her around. I used to see her on the grounds in the morning . . . laughing at trees, at flowers, at little stones . . .

ROBERT. [A burst of laughter] Well, it **is** funny. In humor, so often there's an **irrational** factor. Sometimes, that's what makes it funny. And insanity is irrational. So, what are we to do? -- stop laughing? [Pause, sobered] What happened to her -- your laughing woman?

CLAIRE. Well, they couldn't stop her. She became skin and bones . . . the cheeks all hollowed . . . the eyes . . . She was a skeleton sitting in a wheelchair, but the little shoulders were still hunched over and shaking with silent laughter. Stones . . . flowers . . . [ROBERT kisses her cheek] Leaves blowing along the walk.

ROBERT. [Kisses her again, feels her head] You feel warm.

[JOHN enters -- a little boy in grey, with a toy boat. He wanders slowly around, stylized, staying in the background, in a kind of self-absorbed reverie, fussing with, occasionally sailing his boat in the air.]

CLAIRE. [Oblivious] Do I? My throat's scratchy. Bob, if I **were** a medium . . . [Pause] I've gone to seances. They were -- dreary, most of them, with some frowsy woman writhing and mumbling in the dark. Once I saw ectoplasm, they said it was, a white cord of it hanging in the air. I suppose it could have been fake, but it seemed to flow from the medium's body. And it's this -- substance, you know, that the . . . spirit uses when it materializes. [Pause, ROBERT walks away, disturbed] Another time . . . just after Jamie's death . . .

ROBERT. [Low warning] Claire--!

CLAIRE. [Undeterred] I went to a medium and she spoke to me in Jamie's voice. Jamie's voice, Robert. [Angry, sharp, as if ROBERT were denying the possibility] Do you think I don't **know** my son! Do you think I can't tell **his** voice from **ten thousand others**! [With great longing, movingly] It was faint . . . so far away at first, and mixed with it somehow, were the circumstances of his death. I heard the sea, Bobby, the way it was that day . . . the waves breaking with that sharp and thunderous crack that means the tide is high . . . [Pause, recovering from being drawn into the memory] This -- medium told me that after a sudden death, anything violent, like suicide, or an accident, the soul sustains a shock; it can't make the transition, or realize its new sense of time and conditions. It clings to its previous life, dazed and disoriented. And if that's true, I suppose that's why Jamie . . .

ROBERT. Enough! I don't want to hear anymore.

CLAIRE. All right. I won't talk about it. I'll just . . . say his name, over and over. [Sadly, sweetly] Jamie . . . Jamie . . . Jamie . . . Sometimes I think **that** word is the sweetest in all the world.

ROBERT. No sweeter than Bill, or George, or John.

MOTHER. [Off, calling] John -- ?

[JOHN exits.]

CLAIRE. [Looking up, reminded of them] John?

ROBERT. You're no different from all the other women in the world who lost a son, and faced it with -- dignity. With grief, sure, God with grief, but not . . .

CLAIRE. [Looks at, fingers her wrists] Suicide is undignified. [Laughs] No. You're wrong. I'm -- **me**, not all the other **brave** women in the world, whoever they are. Each one of us has a different capacity for pain; there are degrees of sensitivity to suffering, just as there are to love.

ROBERT. Your endowment, I take it, was great.

CLAIRE. [Shrugs] I was willing to learn that much at the hospital. [She begins to listen intently.]

ROBERT. [Turning away] But not how to heal yourself. Even when Jamie was alive, there was something tragic between the two of you. What you had going was not only a conspiracy, it was a full-blown mystique.

CLAIRE. With a five year-old boy! [She laughs, and JOHN and JESSICA offstage join in her laughter -- all of it seeming to come out of her. This illusion is reinforced with a second coincidence; when CLAIRE suddenly claps her hand over her mouth, all laughter stops instantly.]

ROBERT. [Turning back, annoyed] There are times when you're as Victorian as this house. What we're discussing, my darling . . . [She is frozen, listening] . . is the worst, the most damaging kind of possessive love. **What** are you doing?

CLAIRE. Doing? I'm listening.

ROBERT. Not to me. To what?

CLAIRE. [As if he were an idiot] To **what**?! [Like a whiplash] Why to **them**, of course . . . **them! them! them!** Can't you see it on my face? They're **back**, they're **in** the house!

ROBERT. There's **nothing** in the house, Claire. You hear yourself, the voices belong to you . . . imagining something you can't have . . . children, a family. Claire, sweetheart, again and again, the answer is always the same: one word, Jamie. Accept his death!

CLAIRE. No! Jamie isn't dead. Not really. Nothing dies, Robert. 'A rose that blooms once, blooms forever.' If I have a religion, it's that time is an illusion. [Earnestly and emotionally, trying to express something complicated in simple words] In this world, we must tick off our lives second by second, event by separate event. We're like . . . people on a train, able to see only a tiny segment of time's landscape as we pass. But, the landscape is there . . . spread out in either direction, past and future, everything in it, breathing, living, **alive** simultaneously. But in death, we're free and can experience time as it is: whole. We can move backward and forward, from past to future, from future to past . . . reliving, recreating every event of our lives!

ROBERT. I see. **Anything** to keep Jamie alive, in some nether world where one day you'll join him. Claire, there are no voices. The house is empty.

CLAIRE. [Adamant] No. You don't understand. It's real. And it **is** in the house. There's another life here, from another time; something . . . [Hesitating] Last night, when you went upstairs, I saw a lit --- I didn't tell you . . . Oh! How can I tell you? You look at me with those eyes, those clear, clear eyes, and I feel ashamed . . . like I was faking, or making up a monstrous lie just to hurt you . . . make you suffer, and suffer . . . because of Jamie . . . [Having become more and more hysterical] . . . because you **are** to blame . . . **you**, Robert . . . not me . . .

ROBERT. [Grabbing her, shaking her] He fell! He slipped! It wasn't your fault, or mine! We went to the beach all the time . . . there wasn't any danger . . . but he climbed where he was told not to climb. Now for God's sake will you understand that, and accept it, and stop killing yourself, **and** me?! [He holds her, stroking and petting her until her crying stops and she is calm. She pushes herself away, drying her tears.]

CLAIRE. Well -- I guess I have my answer. **Your** answer.

ROBERT. To what?

CLAIRE. Well--! If I'm **not** a medium, and the house **is** empty . . . then I'm crazy, Yes, Dr. Williams?

ROBERT. [Hedging] I think you're exhausted, upset . . .

CLAIRE. [With growing vitality and eclat] Oh, **please**! Skip the euphemisms. I'm insane, mad! They're going to come back, I promise you that, and you'll **see** them and **hear** them just like I do! I can't stop them, and you can't either . . . not with all your silliness and cheering up! Say it! -- let me hear those plain and honest words! I'm as . . . looney as a moon-eater! [Disheveling her hair] 'Oh, I'm off to the mountain, after the moon . . . She's caught in a dead fir tree . . .' Do you remember that, Bobby? 'Like a great pale apple is she . . . '

[As she speaks, ROBERT spins and runs out the exterior door, not noticing CLAIRE acts out as she recites, with lovely mad gestures.]

'I will leap, and I will catch her with quick, cold hands . . .

And carry her home in my sack . . . I will set her down safe on the oaken bench . . . That stands at the chimney back . .' Do you like that? Shall I go on? [Laughs madly] 'And then I will sit by the fire all night . . . I will sit by the fire all day . . . I will gnaw at the moon to my heart's delight . . . . 'Til I gnnnnnaaaawww her slowly away . . . ' [She turns and looks after ROBERT sadly, utterly sane --] 'Til I gnaw her, slowly away . . .'

THE VOICES. [Off, faint laughter. CLAIRE looks up.]

[ROBERT runs in from outdoors with his hands filled with snow.]

ROBERT. [Much energy, terrified for CLAIRE] Would you like some snow? Or do you want it melted?

CLAIRE. [Very calm] We're going to poison ourselves, drinking that filthy snow.

ROBERT. Have some wine. It's not bad.

CLAIRE. From a broken bottle?

ROBERT. I strained it last night.

CLAIRE. Through what?

ROBERT. A pair of wool sox.

CLAIRE. [Coming around] You didn't!

ROBERT. The sox were clean -- weren't they? -- right out of your case.

CLAIRE. [Holding his hands] I don't know whether to laugh or cry. Why is everything so wrong? I feel . . . in transition, as if everything inside of me were dislocated, in stress. I don't know what I'm doing here, or why we left home? Why did we, Robert? What a silly thing to do. I'm thirsty. And my hands are filthy -- look at them, Robert. I'm going to wash with the snow-water. You said there was a mirror upstairs. Could you bring it down?

ROBERT. [Relief, she is under control] Well, I suppose I could try. [He starts to exit, teasing her gently as he goes] 'Mirror, mirror on the wall . . . Who is the most beautiful of all . . .? [Bowing slightly] 'Tis you, Fair Queen, of that I'm sure . . . You're filled with glamour and . . . allure . . . Of all the ladies in the land . . . Even though you've dirty hand . . . z z z. . . You are, by far, the best -- **most** rare . . . My lovely, lovely, Lady Claire . . . '

[He exits. Alone, CLAIRE now expresses what she has suppressed while ROBERT was there. She may touch cheeks and forehead as if she has a fever, stare about in a dazed manner, look at the snow water etc.]

JESSICA. [Off] How can you be so silly. Mother, look! A green moon! [CLAIRE is instantly listening]
JOHN. [Off] It isn't! It's yellow!
JESSICA. [Off] He still doesn't know his colors!
MOTHER. [Off] Oh, stop it! Both of you. You've done nothing but argue all day. I'm tired of it. John, show me what you've drawn.

[CLAIRE creeps about the room in a strange manner, hugging the walls, trying to locate the voices. ROBERT enters with mirror, sees her, watches in amazement.]

MOTHER. [Off] I think you're going to be an artist.
ROBERT. Claire --!
JESSICA. [Off] I'm going to be a singer . . .
CLAIRE. Listen! Listen!
JESSICA. [Off] I learned a new song the other day.
CLAIRE. A song!
MOTHER. [Off] Did you? Sing it, darling.
JESSICA. [Off] I'm saving it for John's birthday.
CLAIRE. John's birthday!
ROBERT. Stop it! [He puts down the mirror.]
MOTHER. [Off] I can't wait for tomorrow. It's much too long.
CLAIRE. Tomorrow! Did you hear?

ROBERT. [Seizing her roughly] There's nothing to hear! [JESSICA begins to sing offstage, underscoring scene softly until she comes up full as indicated. The song can be a few stanzas from any folk ballad, preferably with a haunting or eerie melody.]

CLAIRE. So clear, so plain! I can't stand it!

ROBERT. [Shaking her] Will you stop, damn it! [They struggle wildly. She escapes him and would rush outdoors, but he drags her back, pushing her roughly into a chair.] Now sit there -- and behave like a woman! -- not a mindless child. Voices! Songs, Apparations! What's next? -- another razor!? [He strides about the room, kicking, throwing over furniture.] The house is empty! Empty! [Shouting to the rafters] **Emmmmmmmmpty**! [ABRUPT SILENCE. Then faintly, eerily, gathering sweetness, power, JESSICA's song comes up. ROBERT turns slowly and looks up and about -- obviously hearing the child's voice, his expression one of growing astonishment. The lights begin to dim. As ROBERT listens, he reaches slowly for CLAIRE's hand.]

BLACKOUT

SCENE III

AT RISE OF CURTAIN: It is evening. The lights come up. CLAIRE is lying on the couch, her coat thrown over her, asleep. ROBERT sits on the floor beside her, lightly dozing. The light is concentrated on the two, the rest of the stage in darkness.

CLAIRE. [Restless, fevered, waking] Bobby!

ROBERT. I'm here.

CLAIRE. [Relief] Oh! I was dreaming. [Looking about] Was there anything? Did you hear anything else?

ROBERT. The wind. The house . . . creaking. The fire. You - snoring.

CLAIRE. [Small laugh, vain to the last] I **don't**. Women **never** snore. You know that -- even if they do. [Listening] That's strange.

ROBERT. Claire, don't.

CLAIRE. Yes! I must! Shhh! [Pause] I don't hear anything. Yet -- they **are** in the house, close, maybe right in this room. Oh! I don't feel well. My throat. If only I could sleep. [She tries to settle back.] What were we talking about? [She closes her eyes.]

ROBERT. [Resting, closing his eyes too] Oh, -- St. Thomas. You were telling me how much you'd like to go back, and I said, why not? [CLAIRE is asleep.] Why shouldn't we? We'll spend the whole summer there. Every blessed golden day. We'll rent a jeep with a little bright awning, and drive up into the hills, and lie in the sun . . .

[The OTHERS are already on stage, covered in black robes which they gradually drop, becoming visible or, as an alternative, they enter in a suitably stylized manner, barely visible, form a tableau, the light increasing gradually. They are seated at the table, the CHILDREN about to play cards, the MOTHER opening letters with a long letter opener.]

. . . I'll wind gardenias and poinsettas through your hair, and find tiny sea shells for a thousand salty necklaces . . . while the spring . . . comes on . . . forever . . . [ROBERT is asleep. Now the tableau of the OTHERS breaks up. They move and talk.]

JESSICA. The queen, silly. The woman is the queen. Oh! He's so **stupid**!

MOTHER. I wish you'd stop using that word.

JESSICA. But he keeps pairing kings with queens. And I always win. It's no fun. I hate children.

JOHN. I'll be a year older tomorrow.

JESSICA. You'll be exactly one day older tomorrow.

JOHN. It's my birthday, so there!

JESSICA. And **there** to you, Mr. One-Day-Older. I think I'll go out. It's stopped raining.

MOTHER. You stay in the house until it dries off out there, Miss One-Day-Early.

JESSICA. Oh, Mother. I want to go out! Besides -- [Abrupt stop and a tableau as ROBERT wakes with a start. The OTHERS are now frozen and standing in a somewhat triangular position. ROBERT is rigid, listening. Then he stands, searching the room, moving **into and through the spaces between the OTHERS** with a frightened expression. Seeing nothing, he comes back, chilled, sees the fire is low.]

ROBERT. Claire -- Claire, honey, we need more wood . . . it's cold . . . [She is profoundly asleep. He covers her more warmly, kisses her sentimentally] Who . . . is the most beautiful of all?

[He exits to basement. The moment he does so, the OTHERS come alive once more.]

JOHN. Did you make paper hats?

MOTHER. Yes.

JOHN. And favors? And prizes for the games? Can we play Blind Man's Bluff? [CLAIRE stirs, wakes.]

MOTHER. If you like. It's your party.

JOHN. I don't want to be 'it.' It's too scary.

CLAIRE. [Terrified] Robert --! [She sits up, sees OTHERS]

JOHN. My shoe is untied.

MOTHER. Jessie -- tie John's shoelace.

JESSICA. Why do I have to? [CLAIRE begins to back away toward the basement exit.]

MOTHER. He's your brother.

CLAIRE. **Robert** --! [The MOTHER stands suddenly, listening.]

JESSICA. What's wrong?

JOHN. Mama--?

MOTHER. Hush! Both of you. [Still listening, apprehensive] We've been alone too long, too often. This old house is beginning to speak to me.

JOHN. [Stage whisper] What does it say? [CLAIRE moans]

MOTHER. There! Did you hear?

JOHN. I didn't hear anything.

JESSICA. I did. It was like . . . a moan.

MOTHER. Yes! Yes! Do you think an animal is trapped somewhere, or somehow managed to get in the house? [The OTHERS move together in a close group. When CLAIRE moans again, all hear but cannot locate the sound. The MOTHER holds the letter opener in a menacing way. Only JESSICA looks directly in CLAIRE's direction, puzzled.

ROBERT enters with an armful of wood which, seeing the OTHERS, he instantly drops with a loud crash. CLAIRE screams and faints.]

ROBERT. Claire! Claire! [He kneels by her.]

CLAIRE. [Wakes, disoriented, obviously ill] Bobby, the phone's ringing! The phone's ringing! Who is it? Is it Mother? Did you speak to her?

ROBERT. Honey -- sit up a bit. Try to sit up. [He helps her. She looks about the room.]

CLAIRE. Bobby, I'm sick.

ROBERT. Listen to me. The storm is over. The snow stopped.

CLAIRE. Thank God! Can we leave now?

ROBERT. Soon, very soon. I heard a snow plow. That means the main road will be clear soon.

CLAIRE. [Struggling to rise] I'll get ready. Oh, my throat! The room is spinning. Just give me a minute . . .

ROBERT. [Restraining her] Claire -- your fever's sky-high. You'd die out there. Wait here.

CLAIRE. Alone! [It takes her a moment to accept it] All

right. **Anything.** But promise you'll hurry. What will you do? -- About the car?

ROBERT. If I can get into the trunk, there's a shovel. I'll dig it out. If not, I'll go up the hill to the main road and stop a car. Either way, I'll be back as soon as I can.

CLAIRE. All right, but . . . before you go, I want you to know that no matter what happens now, to me, to us, I feel somehow, I'm certain that from now on you and I . . . we'll always be together.

ROBERT. There's no need to say it. I saw them. But somehow I feel it too. [He kisses her] God, you're on fire! Lie back. Close your eyes. Now stay that way until I get back. Promise?

CLAIRE. Yes.

[He exits. CLAIRE moves restlessly, opens her eyes, moans slightly.]

CLAIRE. [Deliriously] Robert --? I'm so thirsty.

OTHERS. [Off. Voices fading in, an increasing babble, laughter faint music. An occasional complete sentence or word is heard --] It's my turn . . . What a lovely present . . . . John's so proud . . . See who's at the door . . . So sweet of you . . . What did your mother say? . . . No, Jessica's mine . . . . What a pretty dress . . . Yes, blue . . . It's black raspberry . . . [Ad lib. CLAIRE stands, staggers center stage, wheels, covering her ears.]

CLAIRE. Bobbie! Bobbie! [She staggers about drunkenly, knocking over a chair, then, too weak to move far, sinks to her knees by the outdoor exit. The sounds of the party grow louder.]

JOHN. [Off] It's Jessica's turn. She's 'it.' [Laughter] Tie it on tight. Tighter! [Laughter]

OTHERS. [Off. A rhythmic chorus of young voices] A-round, and a-round, and a-round, and a-round . . . .

JOHN. [Off] Shhh. Shhhh. Let's hide . . . everyone hide!

[A hush. All voices, sounds become extremely faint.

In complete silence, JESSICA enters from L, her arms outstretched, her eyes blindfolded. She pauses, feels the air about her, advances, encounters a chair, moves around it. CLAIRE did not see JESSICA as she entered, but as the child rounds the chair, CLAIRE senses her, turns, sees her. She rises, petrified, her eyes burning into the figure of the child. JESSICA continues to move slowly toward CLAIRE, groping the air. CLAIRE takes a rapid staggered step to one side, then shrinks away step by step until she encounters a wall and is cornered. JESSICA continues her groping, following CLAIRE's moves, until she is almost within arm's reach. She stops, half turns away. Delay. Silence. CLAIRE, in a moment of courage and irresistable fascination, reaches a hesitant hand forward to touch the child, thus turning her in the right direction, but cannot bring herself to do it and withdraws her hand. JESSICA, now facing the audience, her back to CLAIRE, slowly reaches up and pulls down the blindfold. Her expression is puzzled and frightened. She turns very slowly in CLAIRE's direction. And then JESSICA **sees** CLAIRE. She gives a sudden, shrinking, convulsive step backward. A second's delay, then with a cry of terror, JESSICA rushes wildly from the room. ROBERT enters, and seems quite as staggered with shock and panic as CLAIRE.]

ROBERT. [Hoarsely] The car, Claire . . . I found it . . . in a clear spot . . . against the tree at the foot of the hill. [He draws near her] It's a wreck! It must have gone up in flames. There are two . . . **things** inside . . . two . . . charred black things . . . one sitting at the wheel . . . the other . . . . [Moving against her, passionate, dreadful] Mother of God! [Seizing her] My darling, my sweetheart! Hold me! Hold me!

[The lights begin dimming over ROBERT and CLAIRE as they stand transfixed. They grow gradually darker, blending into the background wall and shadows. They disappear when our attention is diverted R, as the MOTHER and JESSICA enter, under lights that grow quickly strong and warm. We see them to be solidly real, of flesh and blood. Even their clothes now take on texture, color and warmth.

MOTHER. [Holding JESSICA's hand, making light of her fright] Do you see? . . . there's nothing here. Nothing. See darling. It was your imagination.

[They separate, the child stares about. JOHN enters.]

JESSICA. [Puzzled, hesitant] But there was something. I saw it.

MOTHER. There was nothing to see!

JESSICA. But it looked . . . like a lady. She was standing over there.

MOTHER. It was a shadow. Nothing more. [Laughing, loving reproval] Oh dear. Oh dear! . . . to be young . . and afraid of shadows. Go on now, both of you. You're missing all the fun.

[JESSICA and JOHN exit. The MOTHER lingers a few moments for a last glance through the empty room. There is a trace of smiling wonderment, puzzled doubt, perhaps a touch of fear on her face before she exits. The stage is empty.]

VOICES. [Off. Happy VOICES. Music. Joyous laughter.]

CURTAIN

MURDER AT THE GREY'S HOUND MANSION
Maxine Holmgren

Mystery, High School/ Community Theatre / 5f, 3m / *Simple Set*
This is a mysterious comedy (or a comical mystery) that will have everyone howling with laughter.

The eccentric owner of Grey's Hound Mansion has been murdered. The cast gathers at the gloomy mansion for the reading of the will. Lightning lights up the stage as thunder and barking dogs greet the wacky characters that arrive. Each one is a suspect, and each one suspects another. Mixed metaphors and alliterations will have the audience barking up the wrong tree until the mystery is solved.

BAKER'S PLAYS

Baker's Plays
c/o Samuel French, Inc.
45 West 25 Street
New York, NY 10010
bakersplays.com

BAKERSPLAYS.COM

STONE SOUP
Anne Glasner & Betty Hollinger

Musical, TYA/Children's Theatre / 9m, 7f, 2 either / Simple Set
2 hungry soldiers stumble on a town filled with disgruntled neighbors. Using their imaginations, the soldiers trick the townsfolk into donating seasonings for their legendary Stone Soup, which they have convinced the townsfolk is a delicacy beyond measure. They con the townfolk into giving them all the ingredients to make a real soup, and in doing so, the soldiers help the townsfolk learn how to get along with each other by working together to create something good.

Baker's Plays
c/o Samuel French, Inc.
45 West 25 Street
New York, NY 10010
bakersplays.com

BAKERSPLAYS.COM